Appleville Elementary

First Day

Appleville Elementary

First Day

by **Nancy Krulik**
illustrated by **Bernice Lum**

SCHOLASTIC INC.

New York   Toronto   London   Auckland   Sydney
Mexico City   New Delhi   Hong Kong   Buenos Aires

For Ian and Amanda,
who have always loved the
first day of school!

ISBN-13: 978-0-545-11773-9
ISBN-10: 0-545-11773-9

Copyright © 2009 by Nancy Krulik
Published by Scholastic Inc.
SCHOLASTIC, LITTLE APPLE, and associated logos are trademarks
and/or registered trademarks of Scholastic Inc.

12 11 10 9 8 7 6 5 4 3 2   9 10 11 12 13 14/0

Printed in the U.S.A.
First printing, June 2009
Book design by Yaffa Jaskoll

Chapter 1
The First Day of First Grade

"Woo-hoo!" J.B. cheered. "It's the first day of first grade."

"I've been waiting all summer for this," J.B.'s friend Albert said.

"Me, too," Marika agreed. "I even made up a dance about it." She spun around on her toes. "I call it, 'First Day Ballet.'"

"I like your tutu," Marika's best friend, Justine, said.

"Thanks," Marika answered. "I got it for the first day of school."

"These are my new sneakers," Justine said.

"Wow!" Marika said. "They're cool."

Justine jumped up and down. "I want to go inside," she told her friends. "I'm tired of waiting."

"We all are," J.B. agreed. "We want to see our new classroom."

"And meet our new teacher," Albert added.

"I heard Miss Popper is the nicest teacher in the school," Justine said.

"I heard that, too," J.B. agreed.

"That's why I can't wait to start first grade," Albert said.

"Me, too," Marika said. "But not Carlos." She pointed to him. He did not look happy.

"Don't you want to be a first grader?" J.B. asked him.

Carlos shook his head. "No!" he said. "I liked kindergarten."

"But first grade is a *real* grade," J.B. said. "It has a number."

"What's so great about numbers?" Carlos asked. "I like letters better."

"But we're going to learn to read in first grade," Albert said.

"I liked it when Ms. Kelly read *to* us in kindergarten," Carlos told him.

"I didn't like rest time," Justine said.

"That's because you can't lie still," Marika teased.

Justine giggled. "I know," she said. "I'm a wiggler."

"I *liked* rest time," Carlos said.

"Kindergarten was only half a day," Albert said. "We didn't eat lunch in school."

"We will this year!" J.B. held up his brand-new lunch box. It was shaped like a race car.

"Cool!" Albert said.

"My lunch box has superheroes on it," Justine said. "And there's a hero *in* it, too."

"What kind of superhero fits in there?" Marika asked.

"One with meat, cheese, lettuce, and tomato," Justine said. "It's a hero *sandwich*!"

Albert showed everyone his pirate lunch box. "I have a peanut-butter-and-banana sandwich. Mmmm!"

"I have sushi," Marika said.

"What's sushi?" Carlos asked.

"Raw fish," Marika said. She opened her lunch box.

Carlos looked inside. "Yuck!" he said. "I don't want to eat near anyone who has raw fish for lunch! Ewww!"

"You *have* to eat near me," Marika said. "We're in first grade together."

"No way!" Carlos shouted. "I am not going to first grade. Not ever!"

Chapter 2
The Popper Stopper

"I think you're afraid of first grade," Marika told Carlos. "You're a scaredy-cat!"

"I am not!" Carlos shouted. "I just don't want to go to first grade."

"Miss Popper will make you," Albert told him.

Carlos shook his head hard. "She can't."

"Why not?" Marika asked him.

"Because I'm a new kind of superhero," Carlos explained. "A superhero no one has ever seen before. A superhero who isn't on Justine's lunch box."

"What kind of superhero are you?" Justine asked.

Carlos crossed his arms. He stood very tall. "I'm the Popper Stopper!" he said.

Just then, Miss Popper walked over. She smiled at the first graders.

The first graders smiled back. All except Carlos.

"Hi, kids!" Miss Popper said. "Are you ready to start first grade?"

"Yes!" Justine, Marika, J.B., and Albert shouted.

Carlos didn't say anything.

Ring! Ring! The school bell rang.

"Okay, first graders," Miss Popper said. "Let's go inside."

"Yay!" Justine, Marika, J.B., and Albert cheered. They ran into Appleville Elementary as fast as they could.

Carlos didn't cheer. He didn't run. He just stood there.

Soon all the teachers and students were inside the school.

Carlos's mom was still in the yard. She had been talking to some other parents. But she stopped when she saw Carlos.

"Why are you still here?" she asked him.

Carlos shrugged.

"You should go inside," his mom said. "They're starting first grade without you."

Carlos gulped. First grade could not start. It had to be stopped.

Only one person could do that. Carlos, the Popper Stopper!

Quickly, Carlos ran into the school.

"I'll go today," Carlos told himself. "But after that, no more first grade!"

Chapter 3
Sharing Time

Carlos walked into the classroom. His friends were sitting in a circle. Carlos sat down between Albert and J.B.

Miss Popper was talking.

"I'm Miss Popper," she said. "I like to go camping. I rode on a raft this summer. It was fun."

"Wow!" Justine whispered to Marika. "We have a cool teacher."

"*So* cool," Marika whispered back.

"That's what I did during my vacation. What did *you* do this summer?" Miss Popper pointed to J.B. "Would you like to go first?"

"I learned to ride my bike without training wheels," J.B. told her. "I'm a great bike rider."

"Congratulations," Miss Popper said. She pointed to Albert. "You're next."

"I got a telescope for my birthday. I can look at stars," he said. "When I grow up, I want to be an astronaut."

"What an exciting job!" Miss Popper said. She pointed to Marika. "How did you spend your summer?" she asked.

"I took ballet classes," Marika said. "I love to dance."

Marika stood up. She pointed her toe and twirled in a circle.

"That's a nice dance," Miss Popper said. "But first graders stay in their seats during sharing times."

Marika turned red and sat down.

Carlos began to laugh. He was glad Marika had gotten into trouble.

Miss Popper looked at Carlos. He stopped laughing right away.

Justine raised her hand.

"Yes, Justine?" Miss Popper asked.

"I like sports," Justine answered. "This summer my daddy and I went to a baseball game. We almost caught a foul ball."

"Wow!" Miss Popper said with a smile. Then she turned to Carlos. "How about you?" she asked.

Carlos didn't answer.

"That's Carlos," Marika said. "He's afraid of first grade."

15

"I am not!" Carlos shouted. "I just don't want to talk."

"You're talking now," Marika said.

Carlos frowned.

"That's okay," Miss Popper said with a smile. "Carlos doesn't have to talk if he doesn't want to."

So Carlos didn't talk.

He listened while Miss Popper showed the class their new job wheel.

He watched while Albert put a yellow sun on the weather chart.

He waited while Marika handed out math worksheets.

And he looked at the picture book Miss Popper gave him.

Carlos didn't say a word until lunch. That was when Marika sat across from him in the lunchroom.

"I don't want to smell raw fish," Carlos told her. "Go away."

"My sushi doesn't smell any worse than your salami," Marika said.

Carlos knew that was true. Salami did smell pretty bad. But it tasted *so* good. He took a big bite of his sandwich. *Mmmm.*

J.B. reached into his lunch box. But he didn't pull out his sandwich. Instead he took out a picture.

"This is my dog, Frisky," he said. "My mom put his picture in here so I wouldn't miss him."

"You're lucky to have a pet," Carlos

said. "Do you remember when Frisky played in the sprinkler with us?"

"Sure," J.B. said. "That was just two days ago."

"That was still summer vacation," Carlos said. "*Before* first grade."

"We can play in the sprinkler after school today," J.B. told him.

Carlos shook his head. "It won't be the same," he said. "Nothing is the same in first grade."

Chapter 4
Surprise!

Miss Popper was waiting for the class after lunch.

"I have a special treat for you," she told them.

"Is it candy?" Marika asked.

"It's better than candy," Miss Popper told them. She held up a blue plastic tube. It had small holes in it.

"Is that a flute?" Albert asked.

"Almost," Miss Popper told him. "This is a recorder. I have one for each of you."

"Yay!" Marika, Justine, Albert, and J.B. cheered.

Carlos didn't say a word. But he smiled a little.

Miss Popper put the recorder up to her lips. She began to play a tune.

"I know that song!" Marika shouted. "It's 'Hot Cross Buns'!"

"Are we going to learn to play that?" Albert asked.

"Yes," Miss Popper told him.

"It looks hard," J.B. said.

"You can do it," Miss Popper said.

Miss Popper was right. Soon the kids were playing the first part of the song.

Hot cross buns. Hot cross buns.

"Very good!" Miss Popper cheered. "You all did very well. Now please put your recorders in your desks."

"But we didn't finish the song," Albert said.

"We'll work on it again tomorrow," Miss Popper said. "It's time for reading."

"I can't read by myself," Marika told Miss Popper.

"That's okay," Miss Popper said. "Today I will read a story to the class. But

soon you'll be reading books by your-
selves."

"I can't wait!" Albert said.

The class went to the reading corner.
They sat down on big pillows.

Miss Popper took a book from the
shelf.

"This is a book about a very sneaky
bunny," she said. "It's called *The Tale of
Peter Rabbit.*"

Carlos smiled a little. He liked books
about animals. And he loved when his
teacher read to him. This was just like
kindergarten.

Miss Popper began to read. When
she got to the part where Peter ate too
many beans and radishes, the kids
giggled.

"I didn't think you could eat too

many beans," Justine said. "Beans are good for you."

"Not *jelly* beans," Carlos said. "Too many of those will make you sick."

Miss Popper laughed. "That's true," she said.

"Carlos, you talked!" Marika said.

Oops. Carlos hadn't meant to talk. The words had just slipped out.

Miss Popper went back to reading *Peter Rabbit* to the class.

Carlos closed his mouth and went back to being the Popper Stopper.

The first graders worked hard all afternoon. When it was time to go home, they were very tired.

"First grade is hard work," J.B. said.

"But it's fun, too," Albert pointed out.

"I liked playing the recorder," Marika said.

"I loved the math sheets," Justine added.

Carlos didn't say anything.

But Miss Popper did. She said, "I have another surprise for you. Someone new will join our class tomorrow."

"Who?" Albert asked.

"It's a surprise," Miss Popper answered.

"Is it a boy or a girl?" Marika asked her.

"I'm not telling," Miss Popper said. "You'll find out tomorrow."

Carlos didn't say anything. He wanted to meet the new kid.

"I'll come tomorrow," he told himself. "But after that, no more first grade."

Chapter 5
The New Kid

The first graders were very excited the next day.

Justine was bouncing up and down.

Marika was doing a new-kid dance.

J.B. and Arnold were on the lookout for a new face.

"I hope the new kid is a girl," Justine said.

"I hope it's a boy," J.B. said.

"You can never have enough boys," Albert agreed.

"What do you think, Carlos?" Justine asked.

"I don't care," he said.

"That's because you're not going to be in first grade, right?" Marika asked. "Except you *are* in first grade. And Miss Popper is still your teacher. You couldn't stop her."

Carlos turned red. He was angry.

"That's not nice, Marika," Justine said.

"I just want to meet the new kid," Carlos said. "I want to tell him that kindergarten is better than first grade."

"You mean tell *her*," Marika said.

"Him," J.B. argued.

Ring! Ring! The school bell rang.

The kids raced into the school. They couldn't wait to meet the new kid.

But when they got to the class-room, there was no new kid. There was only a man. He was talking to Miss Popper.

"Hello," Miss Popper said. "This is my friend, Mr. Furman."

"Hello, Mr. Furman," the class said.

"Hello, first graders," Mr. Furman answered.

"Are you the new kid?" J.B. asked him.

Mr. Furman laughed. "No. I'm the owner of a pet store."

The kids all looked at each other.

"If you're not the new kid, then who is?" Albert asked.

"There is no new kid," Miss Popper told him.

"But you said . . ." Marika began.

"I said someone new was coming," Miss Popper said. "And here she is!"

Miss Popper stepped aside. Now the first graders could see a big glass cage. Inside was a fat, furry, brown gerbil.

"It's a class pet!" Carlos shouted.

The class was surprised. Carlos was excited!

Carlos couldn't help it. He had never had a pet before. Not at home. Not in kindergarten. But now he had a pet. *A first grade pet.*

"That's right, Carlos," Miss Popper said. "She's our class pet."

"What's her name?" Justine asked.

"That's up to all of you," Miss Popper said. "What name do you think she should have?"

"Rover," J.B. said.

31

"That's a dog name," Albert said. "She's a gerbil."

"How about Dancer?" Marika asked.

"That's a name for a reindeer," Justine told her. "*Santa's* reindeer."

"Happy," Carlos whispered.

"What did you say, Carlos?" Miss Popper asked.

32

"I think we should name her Happy," Carlos said, louder this time. "Because she makes me happy."

"Me, too," Justine said. "Happy is a great name!"

J.B., Albert, and even Marika agreed.

"Happy it is," Miss Popper said.

She took out her recorder and began to play a special song for the class gerbil. Everyone began to sing along. Even Carlos.

"If you're Happy and you know it, clap your hands!"

Chapter 6
A Happy Home

The kids raced over to Happy's cage. Happy huddled in a corner.

"Give her some room, please," Mr. Furman told the kids. "She has to get used to you. You look like giants to her."

"First grade is funny," Justine said with a giggle. "Last year we were the littlest kids in the school. Now we're giants!"

The kids all laughed. So did Miss Popper and Mr. Furman.

Mr. Furman showed the class how to feed Happy and give her water. He showed them how to pick her up. Then he gave them a big plastic ball. It had air holes punched all over it.

"Happy can roll around the room in this ball," Mr. Furman explained. "As long as the door to the room is closed, she won't get lost if she is inside it."

Albert raised his hand.

"Yes, Albert?" Miss Popper said.

"Who will take care of Happy when we aren't in school?" Albert asked.

"Good question," Miss Popper said. "Happy won't have to be alone. I'll give you special notes for your parents. If they say it is okay, each of you will get the chance to bring Happy home on the weekends."

Carlos was very excited. Now he could have a pet at school, and sometimes at home. If his mom and dad said yes. He hoped they would.

Carlos's mom and dad *did* say yes. So did everyone else's parents. Happy had plenty of houses to visit.

"Who gets to bring Happy home first?" Carlos asked excitedly.

"I will," Marika volunteered.

"No, I want to," Albert said.

"Me, too," J.B. added.

"And me," Justine shouted.

Miss Popper put her finger to her lips. The kids quieted down.

"You'll each get a chance to bring Happy home," the teacher said. "Today, we'll draw names from a hat to see who goes first."

Carlos really wanted to be the first one to bring Happy home. He wrote his name really big on his piece of paper. Then he dropped it into Miss Popper's green hat.

Miss Popper put her hand into the hat. She swished the names around.

Carlos crossed his fingers.

He crossed his toes.

He tried to cross his eyes, but it made everything look blurry.

Miss Popper pulled out a slip of paper.

"J.B.," she read.

"Yay!" J.B. cheered. He smiled at his friends. "You can all come visit Happy if you want."

"I will," Carlos told him.

"Me, too," Albert added.

"And me," Marika said.

"I can come after my T-ball game," Justine said.

"Happy will have lots of company," Miss Popper said. "She's a very lucky gerbil."

Chapter 7
Little Brothers Can Be Big Pains!

Carlos woke up early on Saturday morning. He wanted to be the first one at J.B.'s house. And he was. Carlos was so early, J.B. was still in his pajamas when he got there.

Carlos didn't mind. He was glad to have some time to play with Happy while J.B. got dressed.

Soon Marika and Albert came over to J.B.'s house too. The first graders sat on

the floor. They watched Happy roll around
in her plastic ball.

"Look at Happy's little feet move,"
Albert said. "She's getting lots of exercise."

"But she's still chubby," J.B. added.

"Are you feeding her too much food?"
Marika asked J.B.

J.B. shook his head. "I'm giving her
the exact amount Mr. Furman told us to."

Carlos looked around the room. "Where's Frisky?" he asked.

"In the backyard," J.B. answered. "We keep Frisky outside when Happy's not in her cage."

Just then, J.B.'s little brother, Mikey, came in the room.

"I want to hold the gerbil," Mikey said.

"I told you, only big kids can hold Happy," J.B. said.

"No fair," Mikey said.

"Happy is *our* class gerbil. *We* make the rules," J.B. said.

Mikey let out a loud yell. "MOM!"

J.B.'s mother came running.

"What's the matter?" she asked.

"J.B. won't let me hold Happy," Mikey told her.

"He doesn't know how to hold her," J.B. said.

J.B.'s mom shook her head. "I don't want to hear another word about that gerbil. You all need to go outside. I have to vacuum the rugs."

"But . . ." Mikey began.

"No buts," his mom said. "Everyone, go out in the yard."

J.B. put Happy back in her cage. Then the first graders and Mikey went outside.

"What do you want to play?" J.B. asked.

"How about zoo?" Mikey said. "I could be a monkey."

J.B. was still mad at Mikey. "It's your fault that we had to put Happy back in her cage," J.B. told his brother. "I don't want to play with you now."

"Mom said you have to," Mikey said.

"No, she didn't," J.B. told him. "She said we had to go outside and play. She didn't say we had to play *together*."

"Fine," Mikey said. He stormed away.

"Little brothers can be big pains," J.B. told his friends.

Chapter 8
Where's Happy?

The first graders were playing zoo when Justine arrived.

J.B. was a lion, roaring on a rock.

Carlos was slithering on the grass like a snake.

Marika was pretending to be a pretty peacock.

Albert was hooting like an owl.

Frisky was a dog. He was chasing squirrels.

"Why aren't you inside playing with Happy?" Justine asked her friends.

"My mom sent us outside so she could vacuum," J.B. explained.

"Can't I just go in and say hello for a minute?" Justine asked.

"I guess so," J.B. answered. "She should be finished by now."

When the first graders walked into the living room, they saw Mikey looking under the couch.

"What did you lose?" J.B. asked him.

"Nothing," Mikey answered.

Carlos looked in Happy's cage. "Happy's gone!" he shouted.

"Mikey, what did you do?" J.B. asked angrily.

Mikey looked at the floor sadly.

"I just wanted to hold her," he told them.

"You took Happy out of her cage?" Albert asked.

Mikey nodded. "I wanted to draw her in a picture. I put her on the floor and I went to get my crayons. When I came back, she was gone."

"MOM!" J.B. shouted.

His mother came running.

"What's wrong?" she asked.

"Mikey took Happy out of her cage. Now she's gone!" J.B. said.

"What if you vacuumed her up?" Justine asked.

"I didn't," J.B.'s mom said.

"You could have," Albert told her. "Happy is very small. She could have been sucked up."

"We won't find her, ever!" Marika said.

"Yes, we will," J.B.'s mom said. "Everyone, start looking."

The first graders searched under the chairs, inside the cabinets, and even in the bathtub.

But they couldn't find Happy anywhere.

Then J.B.'s mom shouted, "Oh my goodness!"

The kids ran to the hall closet. J.B.'s mom pointed to a shoebox on the floor.

"It's Happy!" Carlos cheered.

"What are those four little pink things near her?" Marika asked.

"Little gerbils," J.B.'s mother said. "Happy had babies!"

"In our closet!" J.B. added proudly.

"Wow!" Albert said.

Carlos bent down for a closer look. "Happy birthday, Happy's babies," he said.

Chapter 9
Five Furry Friends!

Mr. Furman said the gerbils had to stay at J.B.'s house for four weeks. Then the babies would be big enough to be in their own cages. When they finally came to school, the first graders were waiting for them.

Justine and Albert hung a WELCOME GERBILS! sign.

Marika did a special gerbil dance.

Carlos gave them treats.

Only J.B. was sad.

"I'm going to miss having them in my house," he said.

"They can visit you," Justine told J.B.

"There are five of them, and five of us," Albert said, "We can each take a gerbil home every weekend."

"We're the only class in school with five pets," Marika said proudly.

Carlos giggled.

"What's so funny?" Marika asked him.

"I made up a tongue twister," Carlos said. "Say this really fast: Five furry friends make first grade fun."

The kids tried to say it, but their tongues got twisted. Soon they were all giggling.

Carlos was glad he hadn't stopped Miss Popper. And he was really happy to be in first grade!

Here's a sneak peek at the next book:
Fire Alarm!

"Five, four, three, two, one!" Albert shouted. "Ready or not, here I come!"

Albert opened his eyes. He began to look for his friends on the playground. But the other first graders were not easy to find. They were very good hiders.

Luckily, Albert was a good seeker. He saw a silver ballerina crown. It was sticking up from behind the bench. Now Albert knew where Marika was hiding.

"I found you!" Albert called out. He tagged Marika.

"How did you know where I was?" Marika asked.

"I'm just good at this game," Albert said.

Marika had been tagged. That meant she wasn't a hider anymore. She was a seeker like Albert.

Marika knew who to find first. She knew where Carlos was hiding.

"Carlos is behind that bush," she told Albert. "I saw him run over there."

"Let's get him!" Albert cheered.

Marika and Albert ran to the bush.

Carlos heard them coming. He didn't want to be tagged. So he ran off to find a new hiding place.

SPLAT! Carlos tripped on his shoelace.

"We found you!" Marika and Albert cheered. They tagged Carlos on the arm.

"You only got me because I fell," Carlos told Marika and Albert.

"You should wear shoes like mine," Marika told him. "They don't have laces."

"No way!" Carlos shouted. "Those are ballet slippers. And they're pink!"

"Okay," Marika said. "But then you'll always trip. And you'll always lose at hide-and-seek."

"Albert found *you*, too," Carlos reminded her.

Marika didn't say anything else.

Ring! Ring! The bell rang. School was starting.

The first graders ran inside as fast as they could. They couldn't wait to find out what fun Miss Popper had planned for them inside Appleville Elementary School!